The HORNED SHEPHERD

By EDGAR JEPSON

Wood-cuts by
WILFRED JONES

Book design by
KAREN MARKS

Address all inquiries and information to
THE WITCHES' ALMANAC, LTD.
P.O. Box 1292
Newport, RI 02840-9998

10-ISBN: 0-9773703-6-4
13-ISBN: 978-0-9773703-6-8

First Printing October 2009

Printed in the United States of America

The HORNED SHEPHERD

CHAPTER I

he brazen glare of the summer day was changing to the golden glow of evening, and the hilltops in the East had already turned from brass to gold. A faint, slow breeze blew from the forest, and now and again wafts of it overcame, with the fragrance of pine-trees, the reek of the market-place, the odours of scorched cattle, the greasy steam of cooking from the tavern, the sourness of sweaty shepherds and spilt lees of wine, the very rankness of the goats.

The bargaining was done: the clamour of hucksters and market-women no longer rose shrill and importunate. A hush had fallen; men and women gossiped in easy voices; and over the low hum of their talk came clearly the pleasant laughter of girls bearing pitchers on their heads to and from the well.

Big Anna looked across the market-place from her casement, her elbow on the sill, her heavy jowl on her hand. Her heavy-lidded eyes moved slowly from Saccabe, the black goat, father of many flocks, who lay sprawled, a shaggy bulk, in the gutter, to the young shepherd who stood so still three paces beyond him; and her brow was knit in a pondering wonder.

Saccabe, the black goat, father of many flocks, was in truth a great beast. His shaggy blackness, the foil to the bright colours of the market-place, seemed now its middle spot, and now the shadow of its brightness. His beard was dabbled in the filth in which he was cooling his rank body; and he munched quietly a posy of fresh flowers, dropped by some careless maid. The while he munched, his eyes, little and wicked, gazed steadfastly at the young shepherd who stood so still three paces from him.

The young shepherd stood quite still, smiling. The rays of the lowering sun streamed full on his face and limbs, warming their smooth whiteness to the glow of gold. His beardless face was beautiful with the beauty of a girl just ripe for marriage, so rounded were the curves of cheek, and lips, and chin. His limbs were like a woman's in their rounded softness, and his throat was as full as a woman's. His hair clustered round his head in fine, soft curls; and on either side, above his forehead, rose two little curling tufts as

Big Anna looked across the market-place.

high and as thick as the first joint of the thumb, very like budding horns.

His eyes were wide open towards the sun, but unseeing, his unchanging smile was the smile of one smiling at an imagination or a dream.

The eyes of a maid going to the well would fall on his face in a careless glance, grow of a sudden intent and brighter; and she would go on her way dreamily with slackening steps and bent head, breathing quicker. A man's eyes falling on it as he talked, would rest on it; and the speech stumbled on his lips.

But all the while the eyes of big Anna moved from Saccabe, the black goat, father of many flocks, to the shining face, from the shining face to the black goat; and her brow was knit in a pondering wonder.

A band of wandering Egyptians trooped slowly into the lower end of the market-place, their faces sullen for that they had reached the town so late.

They huddled their asses together in an empty space, and were unloading the panniers, when one of the old women touched the arm of the chief Egyptian, who was ordering the work of unloading, and pointed to the smiling shepherd. The Egyptian turned and looked at the shining face, and then he stared; then he rubbed his eyes and stared again. The old woman called to the other women, and five of them, the older among them, drew together into a muttering group, gazing at the smiling shepherd. The chief Egyptian turned on them and bade them get back to their work. They parted, each to her task, laughing low with a laughter of doubtful meaning. But he himself gave no more heed to the work, but gazed earnestly at the smiling shepherd, and his brow was knit in a pondering wonder.

The shepherd stood quite still, smiling at an imagination or a dream.

There came a gentle tinkling of bells and bridles; and the Princess, hawk on wrist, rode at foot's pace into the bottom of the market-place. At her bridle-hand rode the wandering knight from over the sea; and hard on his horse's heels rode his broad, squat Ethiopian servant. The crowd in the market-place doffed their caps; and strangers said, "Body of Bacchus, a fair wench!"; and the men of the town said, "Ay, God bless her pretty face"; but the women said nothing.

Of a sudden the Princess reined in her horse in the middle of the market-place, and sat very still in her saddle gazing at the smiling shepherd. The wandering knight also checked his horse, looked where she looked, and cried, "By the tears of St. Elemy, an image of the image, the white image sent by the Prince!"

The Ethiopian reined in his horse, and looked also at the shepherd. He jerked in his saddle; and there came a harsh, clicking mutter from his throat.

But the Princess sat quite still, her full lips, so scarlet, parted, and the glow of a dark fire in her heavy-lidded eyes, gazing at the smiling shepherd.

Big Anna looked from the shepherd to the Princess, from the Princess to the shepherd; then she looked at Saccabe, the black goat, father of many flocks. A slow smile curved her lips, a smile doubtful, like the laughter of the Egyptians.

The Egyptian looked from the shepherd to the Princess, from the Princess to the shepherd, and his pondering wonder changed slowly to understanding.

The folk in the market-place looked from the Princess to the shepherd with the dim pleasure of those that look on beauty and know not what they see.

But the wandering knight looked at the Princess.

And the Ethiopian looked at the shepherd.

And Saccabe, the black goat, father of many flocks, munching the posy of fresh flowers, looked at the shepherd.

There came a clattering of hoofs, a jingling of bits and stirrups and trappings, and a band of ladies and knights and falconers rode swiftly into the market-place chattering and laughing. They reined in their horses with a clattering jingle behind the halted Princess; and were silent.

Their jingling clatter awoke the shepherd from his imagination or his dream. He turned his eyes from the sun and gazed into the eyes of the Princess, and as he gazed slowly his smile changed to the smile of a child awaking in its mother's arms, to the smile of a lover awaking in the arms of the beloved. And the dark fire died out of the eyes of the Princess, and they were humid, and she smiled back to the shepherd, and her lips quivered.

All the folk smiled with them, not knowing why they smiled, and their voices hushed.

When she had smiled at the shepherd, the eyes of the Princess, as though drawn by influence, moved round the market-place until they met the eyes of big Anna, and the eyes of the shepherd and of the people moved with the eyes of the Princess. Big Anna was smiling still her doubtful smile, but when all eyes turned upon her, as if they urged her, and scarce knowing what she did, she threw up her hand across her bosom in the secret sign, the old sign, and let it fall again, all as swift as a flash of light, so that only those who knew the sign saw it.

The lips of the Princess parted again, and a flush of scarlet stained the ivory of her face. One of her ladies, buxom and of a wanton air, smothered a laugh. Some of the townsfolk gasped as at a profaning of the hidden things. The Egyptian smiled. The strange, doubtful laughter of the East broke softly from some of his women. An uncouth word clicked in the Ethiopian's throat.

But the young shepherd stood with the knitted brows of one trying to call to mind a thing known long ago, and long ago forgotten.

There came a burst of loud laughter from the roisterers in the tavern.

The Princess looked once again at the young shepherd, spurred her horse, and rode on towards the palace. Her train followed her. The folk fell to their talk again, the Egyptians to their work. Big Anna withdrew from her casement.

Two shepherds came out of the tavern, a wineskin under the arm of either, and strode across the market-place to the young shepherd. The one, bald and very fat, babbled as he came, full of wine and drunken laughter. The eyes of the other, a gray man and lean, were full of perplexity always; they sought the face of the young shepherd in a perpetual question.

"Let us be going; the sun is setting, and the way is long," said the young shepherd, and his voice was sweet and clear as a girl's.

"Hark to him!" grumbled the gray shepherd.

"He bids me come and go, as if he were the father and I the son."

The fat, bald shepherd laughed and said, "It may be — it may be — who knows? Women are a chancy folk."

"Come," said the young shepherd. And he turned towards the forest.

"Pipe to us! Pipe!" cried the fat, bald shepherd. "Pipe to us the tune of the white image! It will go with the singing of the wine in my head, and I shall dance all the long road."

The young shepherd turned his head and smiled at him. Then he drew a long, slender pipe from his girdle, put it to his lips, and set out towards the forest.

The liquid, joyous notes poured from the pipe in a fantastic, strange tune, full of moonlight and lazily blinking stars, and warm odours of flowers in the night, and burning lips, and humid eyes ashine, and hushed, murmuring voices, and cries of triumph on tall hills.

The folk at the nearer end of the market-place stopped their talk to listen. The girls at the well set down their pitchers, and leaned forward looking after the young shepherd. And big Anna came again to her casement.

Saccabe, the black goat, father of many flocks, raised his head to look after the departing shepherds. When the cries of triumph on tall hills shrilled out from the pipe, he bleated, scrambled to his feet, and walked quickly after them. A man ran out of the throng, overtook him, and belabouring him with a stick, tried to turn him back. Saccabe turned on him; butted him sprawling across the road; and galloped after the shepherds.

The folk in the market-place laughed and mocked at the fallen man. He sat up in the dust, shaking his fist at his flying beast, and cried, "Ah, cursed goat! Cursed goat!"

CHAPTER II

ot half the circle of the moon was filled, yet the market-place was of a very white brightness in its light, and the shadows of the houses lay very black on the ground. The wind from the forest had stilled soon after sunset, and the air was hot, and heavy, and stale, so that the folk groaned and muttered in their sleep. The flame of the camp-fire of the Egyptians, on the side of the road to the forest, rose straight in the still air.

Long after the lamps had been quenched, and the hum of the folk talking had ceased, big Anna sat at her casement with wakeful eyes. Now and again a figure, furtive with muffled face, came stealing along in the shadow of the houses, and stood for a while whispering with her: wives from the sides of sleeping husbands, maids from lonely beds. Twice or thrice they laughed softly as they whispered. Once a soldier in glittering corselet, Olaf of the Northern land, the Captain of the Guard of the Princess, strode down the street from the palace, his sword clinking against his spur, and leaning into big Anna's chamber, talked with her. His loud laugh rolled echoing among the muttering houses.

He went laughing, and for an hour no one came. But still big Anna sat at her casement, and now and again she drank a draught of wine from the cup at her elbow. Then, on silent feet, came the Egyptian.

He was about to knock at her door when he saw the glimmer of her eyes, and said softly, "You are wakeful, mother."

"I looked for you," said big Anna. "The moon draws to the full."

"And the milk is dried up in the breasts of the wheat," said the Egyptian quickly.

"Good," said big Anna. "I knew that you were one of the wise ones."

"And I saw the secret sign, the old sign," said the Egyptian.

She unbarred the door and the Egyptian entered. Then she barred the door again and closed the casement and lighted the lamp. The Egyptian looked round the room at the little shrine of the Holy Virgin, a gift of the Princess, big Anna's foster-child, at the bundles of herbs and simples, and his eyes fell on the basket filled with earth, and the two little effigies of clay lying on the earth in it, among the yellow blades of corn which had already sprung up a hand's breadth.

"I see that with you all things are in order for the feast," he said, and his voice was full of content.

"All things are in order," said big Anna.

"And with the wise among my women. The old knowledge does not die, and the rites are not forgotten," said the Egyptian.

"The Holy Virgin forbid!" said big Anna, and she crossed herself.

Then she drew two chairs to the table, and filled two cups with wine, and they sat down, and pledged one the other, and drank.

"Good wine," said the Egyptian.

"Aye," said big Anna, "the Princess does not forget her fostermother."

"Is the Princess truly your foster-child?" said the Egyptian.

"Even so," said big Anna.

"I see that with you all things are in order for the feast."

"Good," said the Egyptian.

He drank another draught of wine slowly, pondering; then he said, "I never looked to see the Horned One."

"Nor I," said big Anna.

"It is a hundred score moons since his last coming," said the Egyptian.

"Is it truly? To what land, to what people did he come? I have never heard of that coming," said big Anna.

"One of my forefathers saw him in the land of the Two Rivers, a far land," said the Egyptian.

"And was the law fulfilled?" said big Anna.

"The law was fulfilled: the Horned One died," said the Egyptian.

"And was the land rich?"

"The land was rich, and it is rich even to this day. The seed brings forth fruit an hundredfold; the clusters break the vine-props."

"Good," said big Anna, "and the Law shall be fulfilled again, and our eyes shall see it, and we and our children shall prosper in a rich land, thanks be to the holy saints!"

"Even so," said the Egyptian. "But this young shepherd, the Horned One, does he know?"

"No, he does not know — he dreams," said big Anna.

"Then surely he will go back to the hills whence, the folk tell me, he has come, and we shall see him no more."

"He will not return to the hills — never any more," said big Anna, slowly. "The forest will hold him, and the eyes of the Princess will draw him."

"Ah yes; the eyes of Parvâti," said the Egyptian.

"Who is she, this Parvâti? I know her not," said big Anna, quickly.

"So my forefathers called the Bride of the Horned One, and so my people call her to-day," said the Egyptian. "But how if her eyes do not draw him?"

"They will: they will. Did you not see them?" said big Anna. "But an they do not, we will even follow him to the hills, to his home. What matter where the feast is, so that the Law be fulfilled? Yet — yet I would fain that my foster-child, my darling, were the Bride of the Horned One. And I doubt that she would be persuaded to come also. Nay, truly, she could not; for on the Feast of St. John she weds a Prince of Italy."

"Moreover, the home of the young shepherd is far among the hills," said the Egyptian. "He dwells in a valley called the Valley of Fine Fleeces. And the folk say that there are no such sheep in the plains."

"And little wonder if the Horned One be their shepherd!" said big Anna.

"They say, too, that there are no such vines and no such corn in the plains," said the Egyptian. "But that will not be so after the Feast, if it be in the plains. Then the plains will be the richer."

"They will be rich indeed," cried big Anna, and her voice was exultant. "Never did I hope, never did I dream that I should see the true Lord of the Forest. A mock lord we choose every Midsummer moon. But the true Lord and the fulfilling of the Law I never looked to see."

"How will he die?" said the Egyptian.

"That I know not," said big Anna. "But the Law fulfills itself."

The Egyptian was silent a while, considering; then he said, "And the Princess, your foster-child? Is she one of the wise ones? Will she be the Bride?"

"The wisdom is not for unripe maids. But she is my nursling; milk of my breasts is blood in her veins, and her eyelids are the heavy eyelids of those that slumber by day and watch by night. Moreover, she is not all ignorant, often did I tell her the old tales, and once, a young girl, she saw from a hidden place the Feast in the forest. She needs but the telling to understand and be wise; nay, to her the wisdom will come without the telling. Has she not looked kindly upon the Horned Shepherd?"

"Good," said the Egyptian.

There came a tapping on the shutter.

Big Anna quenched the lamp, and opened.

Without stood the Ethiopian, huddled against the wall.

"What would you?" said big Anna.

"The moon draws to the full," said the Ethiopian, and his words came stumbling from an uncouth tongue.

"Even so," said big Anna.

"And the milk is dried up in the breasts of the corn," said the Ethiopian.

"Jesu! Here is a strange wise one!" said big Anna, and she crossed herself. "What seek you, brother?"

"I saw the Horned One; and I saw the sign. Where is the fire-dance and the feast, and the shedding of blood?"

"Nay," said big Anna; "there is no shedding of blood."

"There is no shedding of blood. The law forbids it," said the Egyptian out of the darkness.

"There is shedding of blood," said the Ethiopian. "I must drink the blood of the Horned One. Is he not the God?"

"What wisdom is this? I know it not," said big Anna.

"It is the wisdom of the hubshi, the black man, false wisdom," said the Egyptian, scornfully. "The law — our law — says there is no shedding of blood."

"Truly it does," said big Anna. "Yet have I known the folk of the forest rend asunder a kid at the Feast in the forest, and drink its blood — aye, and once a young wolf."

"Let the forest folk and the hubshi rend asunder kids and wolves, and drink their blood," said the Egyptian; "that is not our wisdom. Our law says there is no shedding of blood; and it shall prevail."

The glimmering white eye-balls of the Ethiopian rolled anxiously as he peered into the dark chamber, striving to follow their quick words. When the Egyptian was silent, he said in his thick-tongued speech, "But the Horned One must die."

"Surely he must die, but not by the shedding of blood," said the Egyptian.

"If he die, it is good," said the Ethiopian. "The land will be fat, full of fat oxen and sheep. It will be a good land to dwell in."

"It will be a rich land, full of corn and wine," said big Anna. "The dwellers in it will prosper."

"It will be a fortunate land, good to dwell in," said the Egyptian. "But I — I wander."

CHAPTER III

n the heat and in the waxing of the mid-summer moon the seasonable restlessness fell on the folk, but greater than in other years. It fell first on the young women, the maids ripe for marriage. They went about their work listless and hasty by turns. In their eyes, downcast and bemused, strange lights shone bright, grew dim, and shone bright again. Spinning or weaving, or grinding the corn, or at the housework, they would fall adreaming over their task, and begin to sing softly a love song; but ere they had sung three verses, their voices would quaver down through broken notes to silence. They talked much with the old women, and round the well in the evening gossip murmured to gossip of love and lovers with low laughter and foolish.

Soon the restlessness fell on the lusty young men, the runners, the wrestlers, the leapers, and the cudgel-players. Then it fell on the young men with bright eyes, on toss-pots and ne'er-do-wells.

The wives were always restless.

Of nights, after sunset, the girls would wander in a band along the road to the forest, and the young men would follow them, jesting and singing love-songs. When they came to the forest, they would gather into one band on the edge of it, silent, gazing into it with searching eyes and listening ears awaiting they knew not what summons. Often they came back two by two, a man with a maid, slowly, with bent heads, whispering. There were many betrothals.

Friar Paul, the lean priest, the preacher, ever watchful, saw that mischief was afoot, grew ill at ease and filled with disquiet and wrath, saying that the devil was loose in the forest. He went to and fro about the town of nights, prying, and talked apart with thin-lipped women and sour-faced men. Also he preached vehemently against the lusts of the flesh, threatening all wantons and loose-livers with many and dreadful pains of hell. And the young men and maidens came from his preaching downcast and fearful, but the old women smiled, for they had seen many midsummers: "Can he bind the influences of the moon?" they said.

The lean priest saw that mischief was afoot.

Then the men of the forest began to come into the town by threes and fours; and their eyes also were restless, quick with seeking glances. They drank at the tavern, and quarrelled. At the sunset hour they lingered about the well, jesting with the girls, and brawling with the young men. There were many broken heads.

One night when the young men and the maidens were gathered at the edge of the forest, waiting for they knew not what, they heard a piping, very faint and far away. It was the piping of the young shepherd; and he piped the tune which the fat, bald shepherd had called the tune of the white image. They listened to the music of his pipe with strained ears; and as they came back to the town, a humming murmur of the melody came softly from their lips.

CHAPTER IV

hat night the Egyptian came again to the house of big Anna. She unbarred the door and let him in. He looked in the basket in which the corn was growing, and saw that the blades were more than a span high, and the little effigies of clay were hidden.

"The time draws near," he said.

Big Anna poured wine into the cups, and they sat them down, and pledged one the other. She wiped her mouth with her hand, and said: "Truly the forest holds the Horned One. He has turned aside from his journey back to the hills, and abides in it, consorting with the forest-folk."

"My young men have told me," said the Egyptian.

"They are a wild folk, and savage, and I like it not," said big Anna.

"He is taming them," said the Egyptian. "Already they follow the sound of his piping, those wild ones, even as his sheep followed it in the Valley of Fine Fleeces. Also he is teaching them strange things, bidding them be kindly and gentle with one another, and even to slay no more of the beasts of the forest than is needful, for they are his beasts."

"Much good will his bidding be when the moon is at the full, and the madness comes on them! Have I not seen?" said big Anna.

"When the moon is at the full, we too shall be in the forest," said the Egyptian.

"Yet I like it not," said big Anna, and she shook her head. "They will teach him the false wisdom."

"We need not fear them: the Bride is here," said the Egyptian.

"Nay, but I do fear, and most of all I fear lest he choose the Bride among the maidens of the forest-folk. They are straight and slender, like young saplings, and their eyes are bright."

"There is but one Bride," said the Egyptian scornfully. "Always there is but one Bride of the Horned One."

"I like it not," said big Anna, and again she shook her head. "Their eyes are bright, and the blood is young in his veins. To-morrow I go to the Princess, to prepare her."

"Truly, that were wise, for the time draws near," said the Egyptian.

"To-morrow also, after sunset, we will go to the forest to the young shepherd," said big Anna.

"That, too, were wise," said the Egyptian.

They were silent a while, then they fell to talking of the mysteries, and of the things that they had seen.

CHAPTER V

n the morrow, at noon, big Anna knocked
at the postern in the great wall which
runs round the gardens of the palace;
and two pages led her straightway to
the Princess, for the Princess looked for her coming.
She sat with her knights and ladies on a shady lawn,
which was cooled to the ear by the patter of falling
water thrown high into the air from a fountain. At
the end of the lawn, under a canopy set on slender
pillars, stood the white image, the likeness of the
young shepherd, sent as a gift to the Princess by the
Prince of Italy her betrothed.

Around the Princess sat her ladies, and the
wandering knight from over the sea sat on the grass
at her feet, and his harp lay beside him.

As she did obeisance to the Princess, big Anna
smiled her slow smile to see how bright were her

eyes under their heavy lids, and how the hot blood surged and ebbed in her ivory cheeks.

When big Anna had made her obeisance, the Princess waved her hand; and her knights and ladies rose, and went chattering to the long terraces.

When they were gone, the Princess kept her eyes cast down for a while: then she raised them, dark and burning, and gazed wrathfully at big Anna:

"I have looked for you," she said.

"I know it, dear heart," said big Anna; and her deep voice was gentle.

"You knew it, yet you did not come to me?" said the Princess; and she frowned.

Big Anna shrugged her shoulders. "To what end should I come?" she said. "I could do nothing. The time was not yet."

The Princess lay back in her carved seat, and her lips trembled.

"I am troubled," she said. "I cannot rest. I cannot sleep; and my eyes burn."

"Poor heart," said big Anna. And drawing a seat near to her, she sat down in it; and taking the hands of the Princess in her own, she fondled them.

"Heal me, mother Anna: heal me, and let me sleep," said the Princess.

"The forest is cool," said big Anna.

"Nay, dear heart, I cannot heal thee," said big Anna softly.

"The leech must let me blood," said the Princess.

"The holy Saints forbid!" cried big Anna. "Waste the good midsummer blood! The warmest blood of the year! Never do that, dear heart! Never do that!" And she made the sign of the cross.

"Then give me a potion, a potion brewed of cooling herbs," said the Princess. She flung out her arms, and let them fall again, and her sombre eyes gazed from under their heavy lids at the white image.

"The forest is cool," said big Anna; and her eyes began to shine, and grew watchful.

The Princess, gazing at the white image, seemed not to hear her.

"The forest is cool," said big Anna.

"The forest?" said the Princess. "The forest?" And she sighed.

"It is fresh and sweet with the smell of the pine trees," said big Anna.

The Princess leaned forward, and looked into big Anna's eyes:

"The forest calls me," she said. "And I hear it calling. Why do I fear the forest?" And she cast a furtive, slant-wise glance at the white image.

"Is it the shepherd you fear?" said big Anna, and she smiled.

A crimson stain spread quickly over the ivory throat and face of the Princess.

"The shepherd," she muttered quickly with stammering tongue. "What shepherd? What of the shepherd?"

"He is goodly to look on," said big Anna.

The Princess sighed.

"His limbs are whiter even than yours," said big Anna.

"I never saw a man so fair," murmured the Princess, and she sighed again and looked at the white image.

"Even the white image is not whiter," said big Anna.

"Why are not Princes like that?" said the Princess.

Big Anna shrugged her shoulders: "They are as they are," she said. "Why do you fear the shepherd?"

"I do not fear him — it is the forest I fear," said the Princess quickly. "I do not fear the shepherd. I do not."

Big Anna laughed softly.

"He dreams of you," she said.

"He dreams of me? How do you know it?" said the Princess quickly.

"You dream of him," said big Anna.

The crimson stain grew deeper on the ivory throat and face of the Princess, and her breath came quicker, and she hung her head.

"I do not dream of the shepherd," she said, "I dream of the white image; yes, I dream of the white image."

"And the white image is in the likeness of the shepherd. Moreover, in your dream the white image lives. I know, dear heart. Why do you strive to hide it from me?" said big Anna.

The Princess hid her face in her hands.

"I burn," she said, "and you offer me no healing."

"The forest is cool," said big Anna.

The Princess shook her head.

"On the Eve of St. John, at the full moon, there is a feast in the forest," said big Anna.

The Princess sprang up and stamped her foot upon the ground and cried fiercely.

"No! I will not!"

"Softly, dear heart, softly," said big Anna, drawing her down again into her seat. "It is the feast of the shepherd."

"The feast of the shepherd?" said the Princess in a gentler voice.

"The feast of the shepherd, of the Horned One. I never looked to see it. The children of my children's children may never hope to see it. It is good to be alive now in this land."

The Princess leaned back again in her seat.

"Tell me," she said; "tell me. Why has the shepherd horns? And why has the white image horns?"

"It is part of the wisdom," said big Anna.

"Tell me," said the Princess.

"The time is not yet come. The wisdom is not for maids," said big Anna.

"Nay; but I will know," said the Princess, frowning.

"Later you shall know," said big Anna. "Maybe the shepherd himself shall teach you."

"The shepherd?" said the Princess. "How shall I see the shepherd?"

"On the Eve of St. John, at the feast in the forest," said big Anna.

"But the Eve of St. John," said the Princess, "the Prince comes on the Eve of St. John."

"Aye, I know," said big Anna, and her eyes shone bright and fierce. "The Prince comes, and there will be the feast of the betrothed. Well, well, a feast in the palace — and a feast in the forest; and the Princess feasts at both." And big Anna laughed. "The feast of the betrothed, and the feast of the Bride," and she laughed again.

"The feast of the Bride: how the feast of the Bride?" said the Princess.

"Do you not wed the Prince?" said big Anna. Her face was guileless, but her eyes mocked.

"Yes," said the Princess, wearily, "I wed the Prince," and she frowned.

"Nay, dear heart, do not look sourly," said big Anna. "A great and worthy Prince, very learned, a great poet, full of sweet words."

"Thin as a sword blade and crooked as a willow-jink," said the Princess.

"Never say it! Never say it! A great Prince! A fine Prince!" said big Anna.

The Princess shut down her heavy lids on her sombre eyes and lay back, still, white and silent.

Big Anna watched her with contented face.

Presently the Princess murmured: "Meanwhile, you have no healing for me. Begone."

"Dear heart, no woman—"

"Begone! Begone!" said the Princess, cutting short the words she would have spoken.

Big Anna bit her lip, and rose. She stood looking this way and that, frowning. Then she smiled, and said: "I have not healing, but I give you respite from the fire. To-morrow, at the dawn, before the sun reddens the tops of the hills, come to the white image here. Lay your forehead against its breast seven times, drawing seven full breaths each time ere you raise it. So shall the fire be quenched for a while."

The Princess said nothing, neither did she open her eyes.

CHAPTER VI

he folk should have been sleeping when big Anna came out of her door into the moonlit market-place to go to the forest. But though their lamps had been quenched they were astir restlessly, and the hum of those to whom sleep is slow in coming rose among the houses.

She stood a while listening to it, smiling a doubtful smile; then she said, "Truly the moon draws to the full," and went her way.

She had gone but a little way along the road when she heard one following her on shuffling feet, and, turning quickly, she found on her heels Mispereth the Jew, the trafficker in precious stones and gold and silver, an old man and wealthy.

"Greeting, mother Anna; you are abroad late," he said, and he shuffled his feet as one ill at ease.

"Greeting. What would you?" said big Anna, and her voice was surly.

"The moon draws to the full," said old Mispereth. He spake humbly, and his eyes were anxious and questioning.

"In truth, the moon draws to the full. What of that?" said big Anna.

"And the milk is dry in the breasts of the corn," said old Mispereth quickly.

Big Anna smote her thigh with a heavy hand, and said, "By the Holy Saints, another wise one! A Jew!"

"Truly, I have the wisdom," said old Mispereth, "and I saw the secret sign, the old sign, and I saw Tammuz, the Horned One."

"Yet another name," said big Anna. "Truly I learn."

"Yes, Tammuz — the Horned One; and at the full moon I go to the Feast in the forest," said old Mispereth.

"Well, well," said big Anna, "it is your right. No one can say you nay. Yet I little thought to find a Jew among the wise ones." And she turned to go on her way.

"A word with you! A word with you, mother Anna! I have a word to say!" cried old Mispereth.

"I have gold, Mother Anna! Gold!" cried old Mispereth.

Big Anna turned again, frowning.

"What would you?" she said. "I am in haste."

"What of the Bride — the Bride of Tammuz?" said old Mispereth, and his face was eager and troubled.

"What would you with the Bride?" said big Anna, wondering.

"I have a daughter," said old Mispereth, "fair, and of a good name, Esther."

Big Anna laughed scornfully.

"I know your daughter," she said. "Fair she is, and of a good name, doubtless. But it were a sorry land that could only find a Jew wench for the Bride of the Horned One!"

"I have gold, Mother Anna! Gold!" cried old Mispereth, and he wrung his hands. "A hundred crowns — nay, a thousand crowns, an you give my daughter to Tammuz for his bride!"

"No! the Bride is chosen," said big Anna.

"Yet she may be changed," said old Mispereth. "A thousand crowns."

"How shall the Bride be changed?" said big Anna, scornfully. "There is but one Bride of the Horned One. Begone! Leave me in peace," and she turned and went on her way.

Old Mispereth looked after her, and gnashed his teeth and beat his breast, saying, "Woe is me! Woe is me! Why did I delay?"

The Egyptian awaited big Anna on the edge of his camp by the roadside, and on their way to the forest she told him of old Mispereth and his petition, marvelling that a Jew should be among the wise ones.

But the Egyptian said, "All the world is the country of the wise ones. There are many wise ones among the Jews."

On the edge of the forest a young Egyptian was awaiting them to be their guide, and he went before them. He led the way down odorous broad arcades, and along hidden paths in close-grown thickets, and at last they heard the voices of men talking low, and came to a glade wherein burned a fire. About it lay or sat folk of the forest, and shepherds, and Egyptians, men and women, young and old, three score or more. And at the end of the glade sat the young shepherd at the foot of an oak tree, his elbow on his knee, and his chin on his hand; and the light of the fire shone on his dreaming eyes.

When the two Egyptians made as if to step into the glade, two foresters leapt out of the shadow of a tree and barred the way with their spears. But big Anna thrust before the two Egyptians, and when they saw her the foresters lowered their spears and cried with one voice loudly, "The priestess! The priestess of the Black Goat!"

And all about the glade men and women, shepherds and forest folk, rose and flocked to her, crying, "The priestess! The priestess of the Black Goat!"

Big Anna crossed the glade to the young shepherd, and threw up her hand over her bosom in the secret sign, the old sign, and bowed low, and cried, "Hail to the Lord of the Forest!"

And the Egyptian made the sign, and bowed also, and cried, "Hail to the Lord of the Forest!"

The folk about her murmured, wondering, then they also cried out together, "Hail to the Lord of the Forest! Hail to the Lord of the Forest!"

And Saccabe, the black goat, father of many flocks, came from among the trees, and leapt among them bleating.

And the young shepherd smiled on them with wondering eyes.

When the folk had hushed their shouting, big Anna waved them back, saying, "We would speak with the Lord of the Forest alone."

And the folk withdrew to the further end of the glade, talking quickly with one another.

Then big Anna said to the young shepherd, "Hail, the Lord of the Forest. You looked for us, and we are here, I and this Egyptian, stewards of the mysteries."

"Truly, I have looked — I have looked for those who should tell me the secret I knew long ago, and long ago forgot. Are you they?" said the young shepherd; and he looked at them with earnest eyes.

"Even so," said the Egyptian. "We are come to teach you the wisdom of the wise ones."

"That is what I would learn," said the young shepherd; "and above all the secret of the white image. From the white image I have learned many things. But of the white image itself I have learned nothing; and I would know."

"What white image is this?" said big Anna.

"The white image in the wood on the hill above the Valley of Fine Fleeces," said the young shepherd.

"Aye," said big Anna, "we will teach you the secret of the white image, and yet another secret." And she smiled on him.

"What other secret?" said the young shepherd.

"The secret of the Bride, and of the eyes of the Bride, even of the eyes of the Princess," said big Anna.

"The eyes of the Princess," said the young shepherd, and his own eyes were eager and shining.

The smile passed out of the face of big Anna, and it grew sad.

"But for you the knowledge is a costly knowledge; the price is death."

The eyes of the young shepherd filled again with dreams.

"That I learned, in dreams, from the white image," he said. "But what is death?"

CHAPTER VII

he white image was but a gray blur in the dusk of the dawn, when the Princess came to it. The waking birds were twittering, and had not yet broken into song. She came slowly, shivering a little, for the air of the dawn was chill, and the dew was cold to her feet. As she came her furtive eyes looked on this side and on that among the trees; for her errand seemed strange to her, and troubled her, and she would that none should see.

When she came to the image, she stood a while gazing at it; and then she looked back over the lawn to be assured that none had followed her. When she saw that it was empty, she put her hands on the shoulders of the image, and laid her brow on its cold breast.

She breathed seven breaths, as big Anna had bidden her, before she raised her head. Seven times she laid her brow on the breast of the image, and seven times she breathed seven breaths. And ere she had done, the white light of the breaking day filled the lawn, and the birds were singing.

Sighing, and raising her hand to her brow to feel if it were cooled, she turned away from the image, and cried out to see the young shepherd standing before her.

He was very white in the white light of the breaking day; and for a space it seemed to her that the white image stood before her, for the young shepherd was smiling even as the white image smiled.

For a while they gazed at one another, shy and trembling, like children afraid.

Then she said with stammering tongue, "What do you here?"

"The priestess sent me," said the young shepherd.

"The priestess? What priestess?" said the Princess.

"The priestess of the Black Goat, she who orders the Feast in the forest," said the young shepherd.

The Princess knew that he spake of big Anna, and that she had plotted against her, sending her out to lay her head against the breast of the white image in the dawn, that the young shepherd might find her, and have speech of her; and she was angered.

But she looked again at the young shepherd, and her anger passed away.

"To what end did she send you?" she said. And she tried to frown but could not.

"She bade me come hither in the dawn that I might see a white image, like to my white image, the image on the hill above the Valley of Fine Fleeces," said the young shepherd.

"Is there then another white image?" said the Princess.

"There is an image like to this but fairer," said the young shepherd. "This image may very well have been wrought by the hands of men. But the shepherd-folk say that my image was wrought by the white people, who dwell among the hills, and in the woods on the hills, and smite with madness those who chance on them, and see them."

"Is it truly fairer than this white image?" said the Princess. But she looked not at the white image but at the young shepherd, and her eyes were sombre no more; but kind and shining.

"Fairer by far," said the young shepherd.

"It is strange that none have told me of it," said the Princess.

"The Valley of Fine Fleeces is far away," said the

young shepherd. "Moreover, none save I of the folk of the valley go near the white image, not even on to the hill where it stands. They are afraid."

"Tell me of it. How is it your white image?" said the Princess. And she leaned against one of the pillars of the canopy which was over the white image. And her eyes fell before the eyes of the young shepherd, for they troubled her.

"My mother found it, when she was a maid and unwed, seeking on a summer's day a strayed lamb among the hills. She rested at noon in a glade in a wood: and the glade was strewn with hewn stones, very white. And some beast burrowing had laid bare the white feet of the image, in the middle of the glade where the hewn stones lay thickest. And she told the people of the valley, our kinsfolk, and brought them to the glade. And they uncovered the image, and set it up under an oak tree. And then they feared it, thinking it the work of the white people of the hills."

"That might well be," said the Princess.

"I do not think it," said the young shepherd, "for my mother did not fear it, but came often to gaze on its fairness by day, and on moonlit nights, wiping from it the stains of the rain, and in the springtime and the summer hanging garlands about it. And when she was wedded to my father she came still to the white image — for it drew her. She came even to the day when I was born in the glade before its feet. Therefore am I like the image; and there be those that call me the son of the white image."

"Truly, that is not strange," said the Princess. And she looked from him to the image and back again.

"When I was a babe and a little child, my mother brought me to the image many times. And when I was a boy I came to it myself, driving my flock, for in the glade of the image is very rich grass. Often the other shepherds strove to dissuade me, but still I came. The image drew me. Many a summer I came, and lay before the image the livelong day; for from that glade no sheep ever strays, so rich is the grass and so cool is the shade. And when I was older I began to dream dreams, strange dreams, the gift of the white image. And my hair grew in curious wise into these two bosses, like the budding horns of a young steer, and like the horns of the image. Now and again at the full moon it seems to me that there are truly horns under the hair, little and hard."

"Why has the image horns?" said the Princess.

"That is part of the wisdom," said the young shepherd.

"Tell me," said the Princess.

"The wisdom is not for maids," said the young shepherd.

"I will know," said the Princess, and she smiled on him.

"Truly, you shall know; but the time is not yet," said the young shepherd.

The Princess sighed, and shifted her feet.

"All of you tell me the same tale," she said. "All of you bid me wait. Tell me, then, of your dreams."

"In my dreams the white image lived and talked with me. And from it I learned many things which the shepherd-folk do not know: how my sheep should get fat lambs and many, and how the corn should grow thick with big ears, and heavy clusters break the vine-props, and the secret of women —"

"What secret?" said the Princess.

"The secret of their eyes," said the young shepherd.

Very quickly the heavy eyelids of the Princess closed over her eyes. And the young shepherd laughed a gentle, fond laugh, very troubling.

"Quench not those lamps," he said, "even though the day has dawned."

"Tell me more," she murmured, and she lifted her heavy eyelids, but her eyes gazed on the ground.

"Sometimes," said the young shepherd, "I seemed myself to be the white image, but alive and in a strange land, among a strange people, and even strange beasts, and very white women. And the women danced on the hills. And in those dreams I learned the tunes which I play on my pipe, the strange tunes of another land, for none of the shepherds, or the forest folk, or even the Egyptians ever heard them till I played them. And I remembered them from my dreams."

"And the white women who danced, were they fair?" said the Princess.

"They were fair," said the young shepherd;" but among them you were the fairest and the lightest dancer."

"I?" said the Princess. And she gazed at him with wondering eyes.

"Even so," said the young shepherd. "Your face was whiter in my dreams, and your hair was black. But you are not less fair; and the eyes are always the same. Even in the furthest, dimmest dream, the dream of the burning land, I see your eyes. Do you not remember?"

"No. I remember nothing," said the Princess. "But why have I never dreamed these dreams? If I danced on the hills, why have I never dreamed of it? Is there not a white image here, also?"

"For women there are no such dreams," said the young shepherd. "The Egyptian says it; and he is very wise. Moreover, he, too, has dreamed dreams."

"It is not right that only men should dream these dreams," said the Princess.

"What matter?" said the young shepherd. "The bride shall not be as the bridegroom; and always in my dreams your lips were sweetest." And he came nearer to her.

The Princess shrank away from him, for his eyes troubled her:

"What is the end of the dream?" she said.

"Some of the dreams do not end," said the young shepherd. "I awake before the end comes. Of some the end is death."

"Death?" said the Princess.

"Even so; it is the price," said the young shepherd, and for a breath his eyes were sad and bemused.

"The price?" said the Princess. "Of what is it the price?"

"Of the good of the people and the safety of the world," said the young shepherd.

"How of the good of the people?" said the Princess.

"That I know not, neither I, nor the Egyptian, nor the priestess," said the young shepherd slowly. "It is the mystery. Yet death is the price."

The eyes of the Princess were again dark and burning:

"In this land you shall not pay it," she said. "I am the ruler of this land; you shall not pay it."

"The law must be fulfilled," said the young shepherd. "And death is but a little thing to the wise ones, the end of a dream, the passing to a dream. If there be love in the dream, what matters death?"

And before she knew what he would be at, he had put his arms about her and kissed her.

For a breath the Princess was stiff, and chill, and white as a dead woman in his arms. Then her ivory face was all scarlet, and she tottered on her feet so that he held her up. Again he kissed her on her lips, and her lips for a moment held his. Then she thrust

Before she knew what he would be at…

him away, and leaned back against the pillar; and her eyes were shut, and she trembled.

"At the full moon is the Feast in the forest," said the young shepherd.

"Begone," said the Princess, and her voice was so low that he scarce heard her.

"At the full moon," said the young shepherd; and he went quickly through the trees towards the postern.

The Princess gazed round the lawn with dazed eyes; then she smote on her brow to assure her heart that she did not dream.

CHAPTER VIII

t noon on the morrow the Princess sat among her ladies on the lawn of the white image. Her face was no longer flushed, and her eyes were no more sombre, but shining and expectant. Little smiles played across her face, ruffling its ivory smoothness as zephyrs ruffle still pools.

The wandering knight from over the sea sat near to her. Once he took his harp and sang an idle song of love. And always, singing or silent, he watched the face of the Princess.

But the Princess gazed on the white image.

A page came from the palace, and bowing low before her, said that Friar Paul, the lean priest, the preacher, had a pressing word for her ear; and she bade the page bring him to her.

When Friar Paul, the lean priest, came, he did not

bow before her as was the custom; for he was haughty and swollen with the pride of his priesthood, and esteemed no man, much less a woman, his better.

But the Princess looked at him with unheeding eyes that saw him not, and asked him what word he brought.

"I bring word of witchcraft and treason," said Friar Paul. "The devil, or a young man in the likeness of the devil, a sorcerer, abides in the forest, working witchcraft, and calling himself the Lord of the Forest. And the forest is your forest, and you are its ruler."

Forthwith the ladies of the Princess made all of them the sign of the cross, crying out each to her saint to preserve her.

But the Princess did not make the sign of the cross, neither did she speak. But she sat very stiff in her seat, holding the arms of it; and she looked at the lean priest with earnest eyes.

And the wandering knight also did not make the sign of the cross. But he looked at the lean priest, and his smile mocked him; for wandering to and fro about the world, he had seen many priests, and liked them not. Moreover, he knew this one to be a meddler and fomenter of mischief, troubling the Bishop continually, haling men and women before him, and accusing them of heresy and witchcraft, and calling on him to condemn them. Then he looked from the lean priest to the Princess, and there his eyes stayed.

But when Friar Paul saw that the Princess was silent, he said: "The folk of the forest are gathered together to serve this sorcerer, who is a devil, and many shepherds, and certain Egyptians, whom it were well to whip and drive out of the land. They hearken to his teaching, a false and devilish teaching; and they hail him Lord of the Forest, which is treason. Therefore, it behooves you, a faithful daughter of the Church and the ruler of this land, to have him seized and brought to judgment and hanged, lest the people go astray. Give me soldiers of your guard, therefore, and I will lead them to the forest, and they shall seize him."

Of a sudden the wandering knight, watching always the face of the Princess, was aware that she liked not the lean priest nor his errand, and he said: "What manner of devil is this sorcerer?"

"A young and fair devil," said the lean priest, "horned, and in the very likeness of this heathen abomination, the white image here."

"Softly, good Friar, softly," said the wandering knight. "The Holy Father has many of these white images, both at Rome and in his houses in the country. How, then, can they be heathen abominations?"

"I care not," said Friar Paul, stubbornly. "This is the image of a devil: has it not horns?"

"What of that?" said the wandering knight. "The learned Greeks who are the guests of the Holy Father and of the Princes of Italy, say that there be horns of honour and horns of dishonour. And many of the white images in the palace of the Holy Father have horns, some little and some big. I mind me that one of them, the image of Isis, a fair lady of Egypt, as these same Greeks declare, has horns like those of a cow, and she was no devil but a noble lady, much abused by her husband's enemies, who slew him. Moreover it is not to be believed that the Holy Father would have in his houses images of devils."

"I care not for that," said Friar Paul. "This horned devil in the forest is leading the people astray by false teaching and witchcraft, and they call him the Lord of the Forest, which is the Princess's, and that is treason."

"What does he teach?" said the Princess; and she looked on the lean priest with unkindly eyes.

"False teaching," said the lean priest.

The Princess was silent, seeming to ponder his words. And a page came from the palace, bringing with him big Anna; and she came, and stood near to Friar Paul, looking from him to the Princess, with watchful, questioning eyes.

But the Princess seemed not to see her, and said to Friar Paul: "What manner of false teaching does this horned sorcerer teach?"

"What matter what he teaches?" said Friar Paul; and his voice was loud and wrathful. "Who is he, to teach? The Church alone may teach. I bid you, daughter, take away this sorcerer, this abomination, from the midst of the people, lest he lead them astray."

"How shall I do this, not knowing what he teaches?" said the Princess, and she lay back in her seat.

Then Friar Paul was more angered than ever; and he cried: "He teaches witchcraft. And big Anna, here, the witch and mother of mischief, is his helper in iniquity, helping him lead astray the people."

Big Anna thrust forward with a very angry face.

"Hearken to him!" she cried. "Does he accuse me? Me who never miss a mass? And two-and-twenty candles of fine wax have I burned since Eastertide at the shrine of the blessed Virgin. O that a poor woman should be so belied! O the shame of it!"

"I know what I know," said the lean priest, frowning on her. "On what errand do you go to the forest, now at the new moon and now at the full?"

"I go to gather herbs and simples for the sick and those ill of a fever. Who does not know it? O the shame of it, to accuse a poor woman and a widow!" said big Anna; and her face was red with her wrath.

"Fine herbs," said the lean priest. "What of the Black Goat, woman? What of the Black Goat?"

"Peace!" said the Princess. "Who gave you leave to wrangle and brawl before me?"

Big Anna and the lean priest were silent, frowning on one another, and biting their lips.

Then the Princess said: "Touching this shepherd, Friar, whom you declare a devil and a sorcerer, bringing no proof, I will take counsel of the Bishop when he returns, conducting hither the Prince, my betrothed. And if it seem good to him, the shepherd shall be brought to judgment, and if he be found indeed a sorcerer, he shall be condemned."

"The Bishop! You will wait for the Bishop!" cried Friar Paul. "Meanwhile the people are led astray. And the Bishop, when he comes, he will do nothing."

"I will not meddle with the matter," said the Princess. "The Bishop shall deal with it."

And Friar Paul turned on his heel, making no obeisance, and went his way, muttering in his beard.

CHAPTER IX

hen Friar Paul had gone from the lawn of the white image, muttering in his beard, the ladies of the Princess babbled shrilly of witchcraft and sorcery and devils in the forest. But the Princess, herself, was silent, pondering with a frowning brow. Then when their chatter had died down, she left pondering, and looked at big Anna, and said, "What would you, mother Anna?"

"Truly," said big Anna, "that foul-mouthed, meddling friar, with his wicked talk of witchcraft and what not, has so troubled my heart that I can scarce call to mind the errand on which I came. But I have a private petition to make for your ear alone, O Princess."

"I am always ready to hear you, mother Anna," said the Princess in a gentle voice. "Were you not my fostermother? This lawn is hot, and no wind blows over it. The Long Terraces are cooler; therefore, come with me thither, and I will hear your petition."

Big Anna smiled, and the last of the redness of her wrath faded out of her face, for the Princess was little used to give her such gentle words, but rather the words and frowns of a spoiled child.

The Princess rose and led the way to the Long Terraces, and big Anna followed her.

When the Princess came to the balustrade which runs along the side of the topmost of the Long Terraces, she leaned on it, looking over the town towards the forest beyond it. And her hair fell about her face so that it was veiled from the eyes of big Anna.

Big Anna stood beside her and said, "Surely, dear heart, the coolness of the white image at dawn has given you respite, for your cheeks are again ivory, and the red blood does not stain them."

The Princess turned quickly and her cheeks were scarlet. She looked at big Anna, but the eyes of big Anna were guileless.

The Princess leaned again on the balustrade and looked towards the forest:

"What would you of me?" she said.

"I bring a word to you from the young shepherd," said big Anna; and she waited a while for the Princess to question her. But the Princess was silent.

Then, seeing that the Princess would not speak, she said: "To-morrow is the night of the full moon, the night of the Feast in the forest. The young shepherd, the Lord of the Forest, looks for your coming with all the desire of his heart."

"To-morrow comes the Prince of Italy, my betrothed," said the Princess. "How, then, can I come to the forest?"

Big Anna knew that it was an idle word; and she said: "It is well that the Prince comes to-morrow. Your ladies will be busy with the feasting and the merry-making, and there will be fewer to mark your comings and goings. Moreover, it were not seemly for a bride on the eve of her bridal to feast late; and none will wonder at your leaving the feast. Nor would I that you came early to the other feast, the Feast in the forest; for though the wise ones be secret, it were better ere you come that they should have drunk their fill of the wine of the feast which changeth all things. If also, the Bride be veiled —"

"How the bride? What bride," said the Princess.

"Bride, did I say?" said big Anna quickly. "Well, bride or gossip, it is all one. Are there not gossips of St. John every midsummer?"

The Princess turned her head and gazed at big Anna with searching eyes.

"I go to look on at the Feast in the forest, not to take part in it," she said. "I go to — I go —" And she was silent.

"I know, dear heart, I know," said big Anna. "And how can you easier see the shepherd and talk with him than if you be his gossip of St. John?"

The Princess shook her head.

"Be brave, dear heart, be brave," said big Anna. "There is no other way. And truly I would not find another gossip of St. John for the shepherd."

"Another gossip?" said the Princess quickly.

"Even so," said big Anna, "else will the Feast in the forest come to naught. Be brave: truly there is no other way. So shall you talk with the shepherd for an hour, maybe two hours; and his words are sweet. You would hear his words."

The Princess bent her head lower over the balustrade and looked towards the forest.

"Be brave, dear heart," said big Anna. "Who shall know you when a veil hides your face? Surely not the wise ones who, having drunk of the wine of the feast, see all things changed."

"I like it not," said the Princess.

"There is naught to fear," said big Anna. "Would I not die before harm came to thee, dear heart? And not only I, but also the shepherd."

The Princess said nothing, and for a while big Anna let her be that she might ponder her words, and no more refuse. Then she said:

"I cannot come to the palace to bring you to the forest, dear heart. I have the ordering of the feast, and if I go from it the folk will do some forbidden thing or leave undone some needful ceremony, and the feast will come to naught."

"Who then will bring me to the forest?" said the Princess.

"There is an Egyptian, one of the wise ones, and a steward of the mysteries," said big Anna. "An hour before midnight he will come to the postern of the gardens, he and six of his young men, bearing a litter. These I chose to bring you to the hidden glade, because on the morrow of the feast they fare forth through the world, and if they tell their tale, they tell it to strangers. They shall bring you to the hidden glade, and there I will await you, I and the shepherd."

"Nay," said the Princess. "Do you come to the postern and let the Egyptian order the feast."

"It may not be, dear heart," said big Anna. "The

folk know me, and fear me, and do my bidding. But the Egyptian they do not know. How then will they do his bidding?"

"If needs must," said the Princess, and she frowned.

"Needs must, indeed, dear heart," said big Anna. "If the feast of the Horned One come to naught, then is the land accursed."

The Princess was silent a while; then she turned a frowning face to big Anna, and said: "That priest, Friar Paul, I like not the lean hound, he will work mischief."

"He is naught — a meddler," said big Anna. "As yet he knows nothing, whatever he may say. But he were better dead, dear heart, lest he learn. I will not burn for a lean priest."

"The Prince, my lord that is to be, loves my land and not me whom he has never seen," said the Princess. "It were well that this lean one should not gain his ear."

"Fear not, dear heart," said big Anna. "The Friar shall receive the reward of meddlers. But I go; for I have to knead and spice the little loaves of the feast, and to make ready the wine."

And big Anna turned and went.

CHAPTER X

riar Paul, the lean priest, came from the palace very ill content with the word of the Princess that she would confer with the Bishop concerning the sorcerer. For he liked not the Bishop; and the Bishop, an old man, gentle, courteous and a lover of peace, who had lived many years at Rome, liked not Friar Paul. To the complaints and accusations of Friar Paul, and they were many, he gave little heed, and when he might he put them by. Heretics he would not burn, but admonished them, bidding them mend their beliefs and forsake the paths of their folly. He would not even burn the witches and sorcerers the lean priest haled before him; a few of them he hanged, and others he whipped and set in stocks. Therefore Friar Paul murmured against him as a lukewarm Lord of the Church, and contemned him as a man of a poor spirit.

Pondering the matter as he came from the palace, it came to his mind that he had done ill in accusing the young shepherd before the Princess; for she would surely listen to the prayers of big Anna, her foster-mother, and let him go free. It seemed good to him rather to let him be for that night and the morrow, till the Prince of Italy should have wedded the Princess, and be lord of the land. For being newly made lord of it, he would assuredly deal hardly with traitors; and the young shepherd, if he did not burn for sorcery, would hang for treason, since the folk of the forest hailed him Lord of the Forest.

Therefore, when he had come down into the town, Friar Paul went to the chief men of it, the Masters of the Guilds, rich, and fat, and fearful. He went to them one by one, and told each of witchcraft, and devils in the forest, and treason. And he terrified them so that they gave him leave to take the Watch, whenever it seemed good to him, and seize the young shepherd in the midst of his sorcery and treason, and bring him to judgment.

Now while Friar Paul was going to and fro among the chief men of the town, filling them with fears, and bending them to his purpose, big Anna was busy mixing the dough of the little loaves of the feast, and spicing it with honey and strange herbs gathered at propitious hours. And when the dough was mixed, she made the little loaves, some in the shape of a man, and some in the shape of a woman, chanting the while the due incantations and performing the ceremonies. And over one little loaf, the loaf of the Horned One and the Bride, she chanted another incantation and performed another ceremony. Then she put them aside to be baked in an oven prepared for them, heated with seven bundles of hazel branches and seven bundles of the branches of an oak.

She had set the little loaves aside, and was covering them with fair white napkins, when the wife of the Master of the Armourers came to her in haste, bringing word of the doings of Friar Paul; how he had persuaded the chief men of the town to give him leave to take the Watch whenever it seemed good to him, and seize the young shepherd, and bring him to judgment before the Prince.

Then big Anna cursed the lean priest; in his downsitting and uprising, waking and sleeping, limb by limb and member by member from the crown of his head to the sole of his foot. Neither Bishop nor Archbishop, nor even the Holy Father at Rome himself could have cursed him thoroughly as big

Anna cursed him. For she cursed him not only by the Virgin and the Holy Trinity and all the Saints, but also by all the devils, calling upon them by the dreadful names.

Of a sudden, in the middle of cursing him by all the devils, she stopped short, and smote her thigh with a heavy hand, and fell to pondering.

Then she besought the wife of the Master of the Armourers to punish her husband for hearkening to Friar Paul, to give him ill-cooked food and sour wine, and to persecute him by day and by night with her clamours and complaints, and sent her away.

When she had gone, big Anna bade her mother, an old woman who dwelt in her house, go find the Egyptian, and bring him to her with all speed.

Presently the Egyptian came, and big Anna greeted him, and said: "We need no more be troubled about the fulfilling of the law; for the man who shall cause it to be fulfilled is here."

"Who is he?" said the Egyptian.

"One, Friar Paul, a lean priest and a meddler. He has persuaded the Masters of the Guilds, and they have given him leave to take the Watch, and seize the Lord of the Forest, and bring him to judgment before the Prince."

"But surely he will mar the feast," said the Egyptian.

"Nay, that he will not do," said big Anna. "For the Prince does not wed the Princess till the morrow of the Feast in the Forest, and till he be wedded to her, he is not the judge, but she."

"Then are your tidings good," said the Egyptian.

"They are very good," said big Anna. "A joyful day and propitious; for the law will be fulfilled."

"A fortunate people in a blessed land," said the Egyptian.

They gazed at one another, exultant, with shining eyes. Then their eyes grew dull, and their faces were no more triumphant.

The Egyptian looked askance at big Anna, and said, "Yet I would it were another. For I have talked much with the young shepherd; and truly I think that he hath ravished mine heart. Women have I loved; but none of them bare me a son. And the young shepherd is fair and gentle, and wise even as a son of mine, had one been born to me, might have been wise. Nay, he is wiser, for I have learned of him. I have talked with him of the strange world I have seen; and of some of the strange things in it which passed my understanding, he told me the secrets out of his own heart; whether he learned them by dreams, or by pondering the little things of a shepherd's life, I know not. But secrets which were never revealed to me, he told me. Truly he is the Horned One. Moreover, he is full of gentleness, and dear to me. I would that it fell to the lot of another to fulfil the law."

"Truly he is fair and gentle, goodly to die. But what of my darling, the Princess?" said big Anna; and her voice was fierce. "Is not milk of my breasts blood in her veins? Did she not hold me with little hands, and call me mother? How shall I bear her sorrow and lamentation for the slain shepherd?"

They were silent a while, pondering; and their faces were sorrowful.

Then big Anna said: "The good of the people? What is the people to us?"

"The people?" said the Egyptian, and he threw out his hand as one who cast the people to the winds.

"Then let the shepherd live," said big Anna. "Murrain and blight, drought and flood, famine and pestilence, an accursed land," said the Egyptian.

"No matter," said big Anna. "Let them love."

"It may not be," said the Egyptian. "The law must be fulfilled. I know not why; we are but stewards of the mysteries. Something we know, and much is hidden from us. Yet we may not hinder the fulfillment of the law. Nay; the law fulfils itself; and, an we would, we cannot stay its fulfillment."

"It is true," said big Anna. "Yet how will the Princess, my darling, sorrow for the shepherd!"

"She will not sorrow long," said the Egyptian. "Surely she shall have comfort and consolation."

"Truly she shall; I had forgotten it," said big Anna.

"Moreover she will have the remembrance," said the Egyptian.

"Remembrance!" said big Anna scornfully. "What is remembrance? Does the remembrance of food fill an empty belly, or does the memory of my husband's arms keep me warm of winter nights?"

"Peace," said the Egyptian; "you speak as a woman."

CHAPTER VIII

t noon on the morrow came the Prince
from Italy, the betrothed of the Princess,
and a great company of gentlemen, and
councilors, and soldiers, and servants
rode with him. But about the Prince, himself, rode
neither gentlemen nor councilors, but poets, lean men
of no account. And at his bridle-hand rode Polydore,
the Greek, a learned man, who helped him seek the
secret of the mysteries, those of Isis and Dionysus
and the Eleusinian.

The heart of the Prince was set on strange
knowledge, on learning the secret of the mysteries.
Also he was a great poet, skilful in quaint
conceits and intricate measures, knowing all
the schemes and figures of verse. And he had
gathered to his court many poets to do honour to
his poetry.

"Swart, lean and crooked," said big Anna

After the poets came his gentlemen and councilors, and after them came pack-horses laden with carved chests of cedar wood, in which were many fair writings in the old tongues. These the Prince held very precious, for they told of the mysteries; and soldiers, picked men, guarded them always.

The Egyptian and big Anna watched the coming of the Prince from her casement. And when he had ridden by, and the townsfolk were shouting, she drew in her head, frowning, and said: "Swart, lean, and crooked."

"The folk tell me that he is a learned Prince, a great poet," said the Egyptian.

"What profit hath a woman of a poet?" said big Anna, scornfully. "The man is lean and crooked."

"Maybe he has a great spirit. Is the spirit naught?" said the Egyptian, and he smiled.

"What is the spirit?" said big Anna stubbornly. "The man is lean and crooked."

"It is good that he should be so," said the Egyptian. "So will the Bride love the Horned One the more."

"Truly, she will," said big Anna, and she was appeased.

When the Prince came to the palace, the gentlemen of the Princess conducted him to the lodging set apart for him and his train. And his servants dressed him in fine attire, and perfumed him. But when he was ready to go to the Princess, and she awaited him in the hall of the palace, he made no haste to go, but first watched over the opening of the chests in which were the writings which told of the mysteries. And he appointed their tasks to the secretaries, and talked for a while with Polydore, the learned Greek.

Then he sighed with a fretting heart, and said, "How this foolish marrying wastes the hours! But all is in order, my Polydore; and you will watch over the secretaries, and see to it that they perform punctually their tasks. Would that you might discharge for me this business of marrying, and I might stay with the secretaries seeking the secret. But I must betake me to my betrothed, this foreign Princess, who has none of the learning of our ladies. I warrant she recks little of divine poetry."

"She is fair, and her land is rich," said Polydore.

"Her land is rich, truly, else would I not be in it," said the Prince. "Its revenue shall buy me many writings which treat of the mysteries, and entertain many skilful poets. But what is fairness if it be not set off with learning?"

"Learning may be taught, but fairness is hard to come by," said Polydore. "The Princess may be taught."

"Truly she may," said the Prince. "And surely this sonnet which I have composed to do her honour shall first open her eyes, so that she shall become aware of the beauty of divine poetry, and grow eager to learn."

"Only a senseless stock, or brute beast void of understanding, could remain blind having heard it, a galaxy of conceits," said Polydore.

Then the Prince went to the hall of the palace, and his poets and gentlemen and councilors followed him. There the Princess was awaiting him, sitting on her throne. Her ladies chattered among themselves, marvelling at the tarrying of the Prince; and the lords of her land muttered with frowning faces, calling him a laggard and discourteous Prince that he should so delay.

But the Princess sat silent and listless, hearing only the slow feet of the hours.

When at last the Prince came and they had greeted one the other, he sat him down beside her on the throne. Then the lords of her land came and paid homage to him one by one; but they did not swear fealty to him till after he should have wedded the Princess. And the Prince was sparing of the fair words which make men friends, for he was impatient and eager to be done with the business.

When the last of the lords had paid homage to him, he took a scroll from one of his pages and read the sonnet he had composed to do honour to the Princess, a sonnet full of quaint conceits and rare rhymes.

And when he had read it, his poets cried out, saying: "O Master! O wonderful! And others cried: "A marvel! A marvel!" And the poet best beloved of the Prince wept bitterly, and cried: "O that I should have lived to see this day! Let this sonnet be inscribed on tablets of gold and set up in all the towns of Italy and in this kingdom!"

And all the gentlemen and councilors of the Prince hailed him a great poet, clapping their hands and crying out. Whereupon the ladies of the Princess and the lords of her land did likewise, giving honour to a guest as was fitting.

The Prince was well content, and smiled, and made as if to fold up the scroll. But his poets cried to him to read the sonnet again, and he read it again.

Then his poets one by one recited each the ode which he had made to do honour to the Princess. Ode after ode they recited; and the Prince sat smiling and well content, and now and again he nodded his head, or wagged a finger approving a quaint conceit.

All the odes were very skilful, full of rare tropes and comparisons and rhymes, patiently sought out, and none was shorter than the others. The gentlemen and councilors of the Prince endured them easily, for they had heard many odes; but the ladies of the Princess and the lords of her land marvelled greatly for a while and strove to understand them, being unlettered; then they fell weary and gaped, for the hall was hot and the flies were buzzing.

And the wandering knight from over the sea sat beside a lady of the Princess, her of the loose lips and wanton eyes, who had laughed when big Anna at her casement made the secret sign, the old sign. And speaking softly, he said, "I like not these artificers. Give me a song of a man and a maid — and love."

"This is the windy babble of lean men," said the lady. "But I suffer it with a good heart, for to-night I shall surely sing 'Sons of the Vine'."

"I know not that song," said the wandering knight.

"It is a fine song, and heartening," said the lady.

"I would like well to hear it," said the wandering knight; and he shut his mouth and slept, for the throne hid from him the face of the Princess.

Poet after poet recited his ode; and the ladies of the Princess and the lords of her land gaped wider and oftener; and the Prince smiled on each poet many times, for he was a lean man, and the heat troubled him little.

But the Princess sat silent, and still, and white, paying no heed to the odes of the poets or the buzzing of the flies, hearing only the slow feet of the hours.

CHAPTER XII

ig Anna came early to the hidden glade wherein they were wont to celebrate the midsummer feast. The moon was yet low in the sky; and the glade lay dark in the shadow of the trees. On all sides many nightingales sang; so loud was their singing that all the nightingales of the forest seemed gathered together about the glade; and in the tops of the trees was a great whirring of goat-suckers. In the brakes and thickets hard by foxes and wild cats and wolves moved among the bushes, calling each to his kind; and fallow-deer trotted along the aisles. The restlessness seemed to have fallen also on the beasts of the forest.

The nightingales did not sing all the while; but now and again they were silent, and then sang out afresh, so that they seemed to summon, and wait, and summon again.

With big Anna came forest folk and Egyptians, men and women, to help her make ready for the feast. Some of them bore wineskins, and some great bowls to hold the wine, and some bundles of branches of the alder, the cypress, and the birch, and some baskets full of the little loaves of the feast. And with them came Saccabe, the black goat, father of many flocks.

At her bidding, those who bore them set down the wineskins and the bowls and the baskets before the square stone which was at the end of the glade, as high as a man, and so broad that ten men might easily stand on it. It was all green with moss, and stone-wart grew on it. She bade the others heap up the bundles of branches in the middle of the glade, where was a black spot, bare of herbs and grass, for many fires had burned on it.

Then the women poured the wine from the wineskins into the bowls; and big Anna bruised herbs, gathered at the new moon and at the full, between two stones, and steeped them in the wine, chanting an incantation and performing a ceremony; and as she chanted, the women stirred the herbs in the wine, so that their virtue passed into it. When the herbs had been stirred in all the bowls, big Anna took a flask of old wine, the oldest wine in the cellars of a rich man, and poured it into a silver cup. With it she mixed yet rarer herbs, some fresh and some dry, some given to her by the Egyptian women and some of her own gathering. And over the cup she chanted another incantation and performed another ceremony, and covered it with a napkin, and set it under the great stone, at the back of it.

Then she wiped the sweat from her brow, and looked at the sky, considering the height of the moon; and it seemed to her that the time had come, and she bade an Egyptian call the feasters to the feast. And straightway the roaring filled all the forest so that the nightingales hushed their song and the beasts their crying.

Presently the feasters began to come into the glade, some by the path and others through the trees, glad and expectant, but silent. Men and women alike, each wore the tunic of white wool, the same that they wear at the feast of the Black Goat; and their arms were bare, and their legs below the knee.

While they were coming into the glade, big Anna went out of it into a little glade behind the great stone; and presently the young shepherd came into it by a hidden path and greeted her.

"Hail, Master," said big Anna. "The feast is ready, and the feasters are come."

"It is good. And is the Bride come?" said the young shepherd; and she could see the shining of his eyes, though the glade was dim.

"The Bride cometh," said big Anna. "Wait here; and presently the Egyptian shall bring her to you."

For it was now an hour since the Princess had left the feast in the palace, and stolen out of the postern; and six Egyptians were bearing her through the forest, and the chief of the Egyptians led the way. Wonder and vague surmises filled her heart; in truth she knew not what she looked for, or what should befall, yet she was fain to be with the young shepherd. But the Egyptians bore her swiftly, for they were eager to be at the feast.

Having spoken with the young shepherd, big Anna came back into the glade of the feast. The folk were gathered together about the pile in the middle; and she also stood by the pile, and all waited, silent.

Then when the circle of the moon had risen so far above the tops of the trees that the rays of it fell upon the top of the pile, big Anna chanted an incantation, and kindled the pile; and all the people shouted together.

And they drank the wine of the feast, and brake the little loaves and ate them. To each man was a loaf in the shape of a woman, and to each woman was a loaf in the shape of a man. As they ate and drank they laughed, even as children laugh out of the gladness of their hearts. Also one jesting gave Saccabe, the black goat, father of many flocks, to drink of the wine of the feast, and he supped it up and bleated.

The moon rose high above the trees, and filled all the glade with a bright light. And the wine of the feast veiled all things with a veil of beauty, so that the wrinkles were smoothed out of the brows of the old, and their rheumy eyes were shining. Even the Ethiopian was no longer uncomely; and the misshapen were straight.

When they had drunken of the wine of the feast, and eaten the little loaves, they linked arms in a ring and began to dance around the fire slowly, singing softly "Sons of the Vine", the song of the feast.

Old Mispereth danced with an Egyptian woman, and the daughter of Mispereth with a young man of the forest folk; and Olaf of the Northern land, the captain of the guard of the Princess, danced with a shepherdess. The men of the town danced with the daughters of the shepherds and the forest folk; and the men of the forest and the shepherds danced with the women of the town, each seeking his unlike as the wine of the feast drave him. And the Ethiopian danced with the wife of the steward of the Bishop, a big woman, and very fat.

They danced round the fire the way of the sun, not against the way of it as they dance at the feast of the Black Goat; for this was the feast of the Horned One, and big Anna saw to it that they did only the propitious things.

Saccabe, the black goat, father of many flocks, danced and leapt inside the ring, bleating; and now and again he thrust out of it and ran round it against the way of the dancers, and then thrust into it again. The folk laughed at his leaping; and the reek of his rankness was strong in their nostrils.

For a while they danced slowly and sang softly. Then the wine of the feast inflamed them, and they danced quicker and sang louder. And men shifted their arms and held the women round the waist; and the song grew a shouting, and the dance a white whirl.

Of a sudden the roaring which calls the feasters to the feast roared out afresh, and the young shepherd, the Horned One, stood on the great stone at the end of the glade, a wreath of vine leaves on his head, and beside him stood the Princess, veiled, holding his hand, and behind them stood the Egyptian, all in the bright light of the moon.

For a breath the voices of the dancers were hushed and only the patter of their dancing feet was heard; and the nightingales had hushed their singing, and the goat-suckers their whirring, and the crying of the beasts was no longer heard, only the patter of dancing feet.

Then the dancers shouted together and cried out, "Hail, Lord of the Forest! Hail, Bride of the Lord of the Forest!" and old Mispereth and the daughter of Mispereth cried "Hail, Tammuz and the Bride of Tammuz!" and Olaf, the captain of the guard, cried "Hail, Balder! Hail, Nanna!" and the Egyptians cried, "Hail, Shiva! Hail, Parvâti!" and the Ethiopian cried out in a strange tongue strange names that clicked in his throat.

As they cried out they danced still, for they might not yet break the ring; but now they danced in honour of the Horned One and the Bride, crying hail to them, and again hail.

And Saccabe, the black goat, father of many flocks, thrust out of the ring, and leapt on to the great stone, and stood on the right hand of the Horned Shepherd. And the reek of the goat was sour in the nostrils of the Horned One and the Bride.

Then the Egyptian kneeled down before the shepherd and gave him the little loaf of the feast. And the shepherd brake it, and gave to the Princess, and they ate of it. Then he crumbled what was left, and threw the crumbs to the dancers as they passed beneath the stone, crying, "Sons of the Vine, eat, and be glad!"

And the Egyptian gave the cup of wine to the shepherd, and he drank of it, and gave it to the Princess, and she drank.

From the wine in the cup rose a tumultuous fume, the sweet fragrance of the heart of the earth, sweeter than the perfumes of all the flowers and all the spices, quickening the body and the spirit. And the reek of the goat was no longer sour in the nostrils of the Princess, but it mingled with the tumultuous fume of the wine.

And when she had drunk of the wine, her eyes were wet with sweet tears that fell not.

Then the young shepherd took from her the cup, and dipping his fingers into the wine that was left, he

The Horned One sprinkled the dancers with wine.

sprinkled it on the dancers, crying, "Sons of the Vine, drink, and be glad!"

And all the dancers shouted together, calling upon him by many names.

Then the Horned One and the Bride went down from the stone.

And the Egyptian came down into the glade of the feast.

And Saccabe, the black goat, father of many flocks, stood alone upon the stone, and leapt, and bleated.

And the ring of the dancers broke.

CHAPTER XIII

t midnight a sour-faced man clamoured at the door of Friar Paul, the lean priest, knocking and crying out that the horned devil was again abroad in the forest, working sorcery, and a great company of the townsfolk had gone out to do him honour and hail him Lord of the Forest. And the lean priest made haste to unbar the door and let him it.

When the sour-faced man had told his story, how he had spied upon big Anna, and followed her to the hidden glade, hearing on the way the talk of her companions, it seemed to Friar Paul that the time was come to seize the young shepherd in the midst of his sorcery and treason, and bring him to judgment. Therefore, he went to the Captain of the Watch and bade him lead his men to the forest as the masters of the Guilds had commanded, and he would guide them to the sorcerer. But when the Captain of the Watch learned that a great company had gone out to the forest, he gathered a full score of the soldiers of the Prince from the taverns, and they were full of wine and ripe for a venture.

Friar Paul was about the space of an hour gathering together this band, then, taking the sour-faced man as guide, he led them swiftly to the forest.

All along the road through the moonlit plain the Watch and the soldiers of the Prince were full of boasting. But when they came under the still, dark arches of the forest they drew together and were silent, even the soldiers who were full of wine. And they went slower, looking over their shoulders into the dark thickets, and making many times the sign of the cross.

Presently they heard a roaring afar off, louder than the roaring of any beast, and they halted, and said to one another that it was the roaring of devils. But Friar Paul exhorted them to be of good courage for the devils feared him, since by virtue of his priesthood he had power over them. They went on, therefore, huddled together and afraid, and presently the roaring ceased, and they heard the voices of men and women singing, and it eased their hearts, and they went forward more boldly.

When they came so near to the hidden glade that they saw the glimmer of the fire high up among the branches of the thick set trees, Friar Paul bade them halt; and he and the Captain of the Watch stole along the path to spy out those who sang in the hidden glade. They came to it softly, for about them they heard the low murmuring voices of men and women; and looking from among the trees, they saw dancers in a ring, dimly, for the moon had passed over the glade and was sinking on the other side so that the shadows of the trees darkened the glade; and they sang as they danced. Who they were Friar Paul could not see, but he resolved to seize them all, being confident that the young shepherd was among them; and he came back to the soldiers.

But even as he went a young Egyptian saw him and the Captain of the Watch, and ran into the glade crying out that the soldiers were at hand; and the dancers, who were now but a score out of all the company of the feasters, ran this way and that, crying out also: "The soldiers! The soldiers!" for their wits were confused by the wine of the feast.

But the folk of the forest and the Egyptians, sharp-witted and used to sudden perils, laid hands on the women and the townsfolk and the shepherds, who thronged into the glade out of the thickets, and drew them quickly in among the trees again, bidding them hush their crying, and they should escape by the secret paths. But old Mispereth and others that were drunken with the wine of the feast, they laid among the bushes.

While they did this, big Anna and the Egyptian came quickly from among the trees crying to one another to save the Bride.

And presently the Watch and the soldiers came running into the glade of the feast, crying: "Where is the Lord of the Forest, the sorcerer? Yield to us the Lord of the Forest!"

And they stood dumbfounded, gripping their swords, for the glade was empty, and none answered; only from among the trees, the voice of an old man cried quavering: "Berkaial — Berkaial — Berkaial."

CHAPTER XIV

Big Anna and the Egyptian came running into the little glade behind the great stone and cried to the Princess and the young shepherd to fly, for the soldiers were upon them. But as in a dream they stared at big Anna and the Egyptian with bright eyes that saw them not; and the Princess drew her veil over her face.

And they rose, and she leaned against the young shepherd, and straightway they heard the clamour of the soldiers, and then no sound, and then the quavering cry of the old man, and then the voice of Friar Paul, the lean priest, bidding the soldiers scour the trees round the glade.

Then big Anna laid hands on the Princess and shook her, crying, "Awake, child! Awake!"

And the Egyptian said, "Come, let us fly quickly, for if the Princess be found here, she shall surely burn

Big Anna shook the Princess…

at Rome that the Prince may inherit her land!"

But the young shepherd passed a hand over his eyes and brushed away the mist, and said, "I fly not. This is the fulfilling of the law. Moreover, it is me they seek, and having seized me they will be content, and the Princess and the feasters shall escape."

And he took the Princess from big Anna and held her to him, and kissed her on the eyes and on the lips, and said, "Whate'er befall, be silent, dear love! Be silent! Farewell!"

But the Princess cried, "Nay, come with me, or I fly not!"

The young shepherd shook his head and said, "It may not be. Lead her away quickly while I hold the soldiers. Dear love, farewell."

And big Anna and the Egyptian took hold of her on either side and led her down the path quickly, for all that she strove with them, and bade them loose her.

Then when the trees hid her from his eyes, the young shepherd sprang up on to the great stone, and cried loudly: "I am he whom ye seek! I am the Lord of the Forest!"

The soldiers ran together from all sides, shouting; and then calling to mind that Friar Paul had said that he was a devil and a sorcerer, they were afraid, and stood before the stone staring at him.

Then the young shepherd leapt down from the stone and stood among them. But even then they would by no means lay hands on him; only Friar Paul, the lean priest, took a rope and bound him, rejoicing. And as he bound him, Saccabe, the black goat, father of many flocks, came from among the trees, and thrust through the soldiers, and butted Friar Paul so that he fell, and would have trampled him. And the soldiers would have slain Saccabe with their swords; but Friar Paul cried: "Slay not the goat! The goat is the witness! The goat is the witness!"

And the soldiers dragged the goat away from the priest; and he made an end of binding the young shepherd.

Then he bade the soldiers scour again the forest round the glade; but the Captain of the Watch said, "Nay, we came forth to seize this sorcerer, the Lord of the Forest! and we have seized him. Let us go hence quickly back to the town, lest his companions, who are a great company, fall on us and set him free."

Therefore they set the young shepherd in the midst of them, and with him Saccabe, the black goat, father of many flocks, and set out for the town.

And the Princess, borne swiftly in her litter by the Egyptians, was before them, and won clear of the forest ere ever they did. And big Anna and the Egyptian walked beside the litter on either side. And all the way the Princess wept; and they could find no comfort.

CHAPTER XV

n the morrow the folk of all the land thronged into the town to the marriage of the Prince and Princess, and to the feast provided for them. In the market-place oxen and sheep and swine, stuffed with capons and wild fowl and all manner of sweet herbs, were roasted at great fires, and there was a great store of loaves and pasties and cheeses, and a pile of wineskins at the four corners of the market-place in order that after the marriage the people might feast.

The town was bright with the many-coloured garments of those who had come to the marriage feast, and with the newly scoured and burnished armour of the soldiers. All were joyous and full of laughter, jesting with one another, and singing the marriage song of the common folk.

Now it chanced that when the time of the marriage came, and the Prince was already on the threshold of his lodging in the palace, about to set out, one of the secretaries came to him in haste saying that Polydore, the learned Greek, had found a new interpretation in the writings which treat of the mysteries of Isis. Forthwith the Prince would have put off the marriage until he had considered with Polydore this new matter. But his councilors were urgent with him, adjuring him not to put this slight upon the Princess and her people; and after much ado he hearkened to them.

But all the while he rode in the procession through the shouting multitude he was ill content, and even as he kneeled with the Princess before the altar he was impatient, frowning and shrugging and gnawing his fingers like a pettish child. Now and again, as the chance offered, he sent a page to Polydore, the learned Greek, to learn how the work of interpretation went.

He gave no heed to the Princess, nor she to him. All the while she thought on the young shepherd. Her scarlet lips were scarlet no more; and under their heavy lids her eyes burned like dulling embers.

When they had been wedded and had come

back through the people shouting and singing the marriage-song, to the palace, they went into the great hall, and sat upon the throne. And about the throne stood the lords of the land and the knights and the ladies; and many of the people thronged into the hall to see the ceremonies, and among them were big Anna and the Egyptian and a full score of the wise ones, forestfolk, townsfolk, shepherds, and Egyptians. And the Prince grew yet more impatient to talk with Polydore, the learned Greek, so that he moved restlessly from side to side on the throne.

Then the lords of the land swore allegiance to the Prince, one by one, and after them the Masters of the Guilds swore allegiance on behalf of the townsfolk, for he was now the ruler of the land. When all had at last sworn the oath, the Prince rose to go to his lodging and confer with Polydore, the learned Greek. But again his councilors stayed him, saying that it was needful that he should administer justice, and show himself indeed the ruler of the land. Then was the Prince wroth, and upbraided them, and wrangled with them. But they appeased him, assuring him that he need not tarry long, for they had to hand a young man accused of sorcery and treason, a stranger and friendless, so that he might be quickly condemned.

Therefore the Prince sat him down again on the throne beside the Princess, and soldiers brought in the young shepherd and Saccabe, the black goat, father of many flocks; and with them came Friar Paul, the lean priest, the accuser.

The young shepherd was bedraggled and stained by the journey through the forest; and his hair was tousled, and the wreath of vine-leaves on it was awry and withered. Also thirst parched him, for they had given him neither to eat nor to drink, and his bonds cut his flesh. But to these things he gave no heed, and his eyes were the eyes of a dreamer, for he dreamed of the Princess and the feast.

But when he stood before the throne, the eyes of the Princess drew him from his dream; and even as he saw her, she rose to bid them let him go. But he said quickly, in a loud voice, "Be silent!"

Big Anna and the Egyptian knew that he spake to the Princess; but all the rest of the folk thought that he spake to Friar Paul who stood forward to accuse him; and a soldier smote him, and cried: "Silence, knave!"

At the bidding of the young shepherd the Princess sat down again on the throne, leaning forward, with her hands clenched together, and they gazed at one another as though there flowed between them a deep, swift flood, widening.

Then a councilor said, "Let the accuser speak."

And Friar Paul, the lean priest, said in a loud voice so that all in the hall heard him, "Justice, O Prince! This man is a sorcerer and a traitor. He leads the people astray, working sorcery in the forest. And last night we took him in the midst of his iniquity, dancing the dance of devils with men and with women whom he has taught witchcraft. And here is the proof of what I say, this black goat here. For when I would have bound this sorcerer, the goat, a devil and his familiar, smote me so that I fell, and would have slain me, but the soldiers saved me. Is not this true, ye soldiers?"

And the soldiers who guarded the young shepherd cried out that it was true; and the common folk in the hall cried, "Judgment on the sorcerer!" and some, "Let him be condemned!" and others again, "Hang the sorcerer: Hang him!" And big Anna and the Egyptian, and the wise ones cried louder than all, "Hang him: Hang him!"

While the people clamoured, the Prince turned to the Princess, and said, "Oh, that I who seek the secret of the mysteries of Isis, and Dionysus, and the

Eleusinian, must needs waste the hours on the antics of these boors!"

But the Princess said nothing; she looked still into the eyes of the young shepherd.

When the people hushed their clamouring, Friar Paul cried again: "Moreover, O Prince, this man is also a traitor and a fomenter of treason, for he calls himself the Lord of the Forest, and teaches those who follow him to hail him the Lord of the Forest. And the forest is your forest, and you are the lord of it. Even when we took him, he declared himself to be the Lord of the Forest, as these soldiers heard."

Then the soldiers and the people cried out together: "Judgment on the traitor! Hang him!" And the Egyptian cried very loud above all the others, "Hang him, and cast his body into the lake!" And the wise ones heard him and took up the cry; and all the people cried as they did, until all were shouting, "Hang him, and cast his body into the lake!" But they knew not why they cried this; only the wise ones knew that it was the law.

For a while the young shepherd left looking at the Princess, and looked at the people, wondering that they raged so furiously against him, since he had never harmed any of them; and the women in the crowd spat at him and howled. But the wise ones hushed their voices; and the Egyptian hid his face.

Then the councilors cried to the people to be silent, and the soldiers threatened them; and when at last they were silent, the Prince said to the young shepherd: "You have heard the accusation of the priest, knave? What do you say in answer? Did you declare yourself Lord of the Forest, and suffer the people to hail you Lord of the Forest?"

"Truly I did," said the young shepherd. "I am the Lord of the Forest. But not as you are lord of the forest, O Prince."

Then Friar Paul and the soldiers and the people cried out, "He has confessed! The traitor has confessed! Hang him! And cast his body into the lake!"

And the Prince said, "Let it be so. Take him and hang him at sunset, and let his body be cast into the lake."

And all the people shouted, and the soldiers led the young shepherd out of the hall, back to prison; and many of the people followed them, jeering at the young shepherd, and spitting on him, and smiting him.

But the Prince made haste to go to Polydore, the learned Greek, and hear the new interpretation, and seek the secret of the mysteries, those of Isis, and Dionysus, and the Eleusinian.

CHAPTER XVI

ig Anna and the Egyptian followed after the young shepherd in the crowd, but ere they were out of the gates of the palace, a page, running, overtook them, and bade them come forthwith to the Princess in the palace.

The Egyptian looked at big Anna and big Anna looked at the Egyptian; and he shook his head and said: "To what purpose should we go to the Princess? We can do naught. The law fulfils itself."

"Needs must," said big Anna; "else will she be wroth with us, and we shall suffer."

Thereupon they turned back to the palace, and the page brought them to the Princess alone in her chamber. The air blew into it through the tall casements, but it availed not to cool the hot brow of the Princess.

Big Anna and the Egyptian stood before her with bowed heads; and for a while she gave no heed to them, but paced to and fro with a swift, even step, like a panther or a leopard which the hunters have caged. And as she paced she tore her bride's veil across and across.

Of a sudden she stopped, and her eyes under their heavy lids burned on them; and she said: "The shepherd shall not die."

Big Anna shuffled her feet, and said, "It is the law, dear heart."

"It is the law," said the Egyptian; and his voice was stubborn.

A bright flame shone in the eyes of the Princess, and she laughed a slow laugh, scornful and cruel; and big Anna shivered.

"The law?" said the Princess. "What care I for the law? The shepherd shall not die."

"The law must be fulfilled," said the Egyptian.

"Hark ye," said the Princess, "you brought the shepherd to this pass, making him the victim. Therefore, you shall save him alive."

"How shall we, dear heart?" said big Anna. "Who are we to save him whom the Prince hath condemned?"

"Where are your devils, sorceress?" said the Princess; and she laughed again, slowly.

Big Anna was silent, and trembled.

"If the shepherd die, you die, you and this Egyptian," said the Princess.

"If we die, we die, but the law is fulfilled," said the Egyptian.

"Yes; you die, Egyptian, and all your people with you, men, women, and children, and babes, a nest of sorcerers," said the Princess.

The Egyptian bowed his head.

"And you die, big Anna: you and your mother, and your daughter, and your daughter's child, a nest of sorcerers," said the Princess.

And big Anna fell on her knees before the Princess, weeping and crying out, "Nay, not the child, dear heart! What harm hath he done? He is but a little boy, joyous and full of laughter. What hath he to do with the Horned One and the dreadful law? Let me die, and my daughter and my mother, but not the little one."

"He dies," said the Princess. "Even now soldiers go to guard your house and your daughter's house, and the camp of the Egyptians, so that none escape."

And big Anna wept and besought the Princess to spare the child; but the Princess hardened her heart, and swore that the child should die, saying that she, a neophyte, might not prevail against the law, but big Anna and the Egyptian, being sorcerers and stewards of the mysteries, could, if they would, prevail against it, and save the shepherd alive.

Big Anna wept on, beseeching; then of a sudden she rose, and smote her brow, and cried, "There is a way; fool that I am to have forgotten it! There is a way."

But the Egyptian said wrathfully, "There is no way, woman. The law must be fulfilled."

But big Anna said to the Princess, "Give me your signet, dear heart, and gold. And I will surely save the shepherd alive."

"Will you surely save him alive?" said the Princess.

"Truly, I will. I will bring him to you this very night at midnight, alive," said big Anna.

Forthwith the Princess gave to big Anna her signet and a bag of gold; and she bade big Anna send to her a potion to mix with the wine of the Prince that he might sleep soundly, and know nothing.

And big Anna and the Egyptian left her.

When they were come out of the palace, the Egyptian said to big Anna, "What is this you would do? The law must be fulfilled. The Horned One must die."

"If the Horned One die for a space and live again, surely the law is fulfilled," said big Anna.

"Surely, if the Horned One tread the dark land but for the space of a breath, then is the law fulfilled," said the Egyptian. "But how can that be?"

"Sometimes the friends of a man who is hanged are well-to-do; and he is dear to them," said big Anna. "Then they come to me, and I bargain with the hangman. Our hangman is not a hard man. He loves his ease, and he loves a full purse. For a hundred crowns he will hang you a man softly, and with a thick rope. And if a man be hale, and I have the handling of him, it is odds that he live again."

"But does he truly die?" said the Egyptian.

"Aye, he dies. Sometimes I and the old women who help me, have rubbed him for three hours and more, before he breathed again. Moreover, I have talked to such an one, and he has seen strange things."

"If it might be," said the Egyptian, and he sighed. "Truly I should rejoice if the shepherd were saved alive."

"Saved he shall be," said big Anna. "But he must be no more seen in this land."

"The world is wide," said the Egyptian. "I will show him the roads thereof and those that tread them."

Big Anna led the Egyptian to Olaf of the Northern land, the captain of the guard of the Princess; and they found him in his lodging whither he had repaired to put off his armour and apparel himself for the wedding feast.

When big Anna showed him the signet of the Princess, and bade him command himself the soldiers who should guard the hangman, and told him how they had planned to save the young shepherd alive, Olaf was very wroth, and said: "Nay; I will have no hand in this. Balder must die. It is the law."

And big Anna tried to persuade him, and when he would not hearken to her, she threatened him, saying that the Princess would be wroth and punish him.

But he would not be persuaded, and said, "I will not! I will not! Balder must die."

Then the Egyptian turned on him, and cried: "Who are you to wrangle with us? We are the stewards of the mysteries; on our heads be it if the law be not fulfilled. See to it that you do our bidding faithfully."

And Olaf was abashed, and no longer refused. And big Anna gave him gold from the bag that he might help them with a cheerful heart.

Then they left him, and went to the house of the hangman, which was without the town; and he easily consented to hang the young shepherd softly with a thick rope, when big Anna gave him a hundred crowns, and promised him that none should see the shepherd alive after he was hanged.

Then big Anna went to the house of her daughter and showed the soldiers who were guarding it the signet of the Princess, and sent them away. When they were gone, she sent her daughter and the little boy, her daughter's son, to the hills, giving her daughter a bag of gold, and bidding her hide from the vengeance of the Princess if the shepherd died.

Then she said to the Egyptian: "Now is my heart at ease. For if the business miscarry and we die, yet is the little one safe."

CHAPTER XVII

ll the day the people feasted, eating the roasted flesh of oxen, and sheep, and swine, and capons and all manner of wild fowl. All the day they drank the wine, pledging one another, and jesting and telling stories; and now and again they sang and danced, so that the town was full of joy and laughter.

Sometimes the sound of their singing came to the ears of the young shepherd in the prison; and it seemed to him the singing of the dancers in the forest. For all the while he dreamed of the feast in the forest and the Princess, so that he knew not that he had been bruised by the townsfolk, nor that he was athirst and hungry, nor that the bonds cut his flesh, nor that he must be hanged at sunset.

While he dreamed in the prison, in the hall of the palace was the wedding-feast. And the Princess, sitting at the right hand of the Prince, possessed her soul in patience, trusting in big Anna. But she heard few of the words the Prince spake to her, and none of the marriage odes of the poets which they recited, for she thought on the young shepherd. And her lips were again a little scarlet.

In the afternoon big Anna came to the prison, showing the signet of the Princess to the gaoler; and he brought her to the young shepherd, and left her with him. Then big Anna loosed his bonds, and gave to him meat and wine, heartening him with talk of the Princess, how she loved him dearly. But she did not tell him that she had agreed with the hangman to save him alive, for the Egyptian had forbidden her, saying that the Horned One must truly taste the bitterness of death.

When big Anna had made an end of heartening him, she came away from the prison, and the young shepherd slept, for the meat and wine had made him drowsy. All the afternoon he slept, till in the evening came Olaf, the captain of the guard, and soldiers and the hangman to take him away and hang him, as the Prince had commanded.

The sun was already setting when they led the young shepherd through the town, for Olaf had delayed that it might be dusk when his body should be cast into the lake. The folk were too busy with their feasting and merry-making to give heed to a hanging; they did but jeer at the young shepherd when he passed by them. Only old women, wise ones, some of them Egyptians, and some women of the townsfolk, were waiting at the door of the prison and followed him. These bare baskets filled with earth in which grew ripe corn, and among the corn were the little images of clay, two in each basket. While they were yet in the town, Friar Paul, the lean priest, came running and went with them, and he walked beside Olaf, the captain of the guard, rejoicing that he should see the hanging of the young shepherd.

When they came out of the town they found the Egyptian and certain of his young men, and old Mispereth and the daughter of Mispereth and shepherds and forest folk waiting by the wayside. And these also followed after the young shepherd, jeering at him and smiting him with the branches of trees, and crying, "Death to the Lord of the Forest. Slay him, slay him!"

And the soldiers and Friar Paul thought that they mocked him calling him the Lord of the Forest, for they knew not the law.

This they did all the way, till they came among the trees by the side of the lake; and Olaf, the captain of the guard, halted them about fifty paces from the lake. There the hangman chose a tree, and threw the rope over a branch of it so that it dangled, and put the noose round the neck of the young shepherd; and the rope was thick.

The young shepherd shivered, for it seemed to him that the dusk was cold. But he said naught, neither did he complain, for he knew that the end was death.

The people were silent, and among them a woman wept. But Friar Paul, the lean priest, stood forward and cried in a loud voice: "Sorcerer, confess!"

The young shepherd gave no heed to him, but shut his eyes that he might see once more the face of the Princess before he died.

Then the hangman laid hold of the rope and two of the soldiers held it also; and he bade them haul, and they hauled; and the young shepherd hung in the air. But the hangman saw to it that they hauled gently, for he stood first holding the rope.

The people were silent, all save the woman who wept.

Presently, when the young shepherd struggled no more, the hangman said, "The man is dead."

"Sorcerer, confess!" screamed the Friar.

And they loosed the rope gently and lowered the body of the young shepherd till it lay on the ground; and the hangman kneeled down and loosed the noose from round his neck, and perceiving that his heart no longer beat, he said again, "The man is surely dead."

And Friar Paul cried in a loud voice, "So perish all they that lead the people astray."

Then Olaf, the captain of the guard, said to the soldiers, "Get you gone to the town, back to the feasting. I will see to it that these knaves here cast the body into the lake."

And the soldiers went their way quickly, rejoicing, and with them went the hangman.

Then the Egyptians and shepherds lifted up the body of the young shepherd, and bore it to the lake; and the women followed and Friar Paul, the lean priest.

But big Anna came to the side of Olaf, the captain of the guard, and said, softly: "This lean priest is a meddler and an enemy of the wise ones and the Princess. Did he not spoil the feast of the Horned One, putting an end to it or ever it was time? Shall there be no feasts in the forest because this lean one meddles? Moreover, it were well that there were a body in the lake that all may see it, for the waters are clear."

And Olaf drew his sword quietly.

When the Egyptians and shepherds, bearing the body of the young shepherd, stood on the shore of the lake Olaf gave the word, and they cast it into the water. And the old women cast in their baskets in which grew the corn, and forthwith some of them brake forth into loud wailing, and others rejoiced, crying out that they had cast out Death.

But before the body of the young shepherd had sunk in the water the Egyptian and forest folk leapt into the lake, and drew it to the shore.

When he saw this, Friar Paul, the lean priest, cried: "What is this that ye do? Let be. Let be."

Then straightway Olaf thrust his sword through the lean priest so that he fell on his face and died. And while some of the folk carried the body of the young shepherd to a bank whereon the grass grew thick, and laid it on it, others stripped his priest's frock off Friar Paul, and tied a great stone to him with the rope which had hanged the young shepherd, and cast him into the lake. And when the water had washed his body clean, it lay on the bottom of the lake a dim whiteness for all the world to see.

And all the while the women wailed; and the daughter of Mispereth, lamenting, cried: "Woe is me: Tammuz is dead; Tammuz is dead."

CHAPTER XVIII

Having slain the lean priest, Olaf, the captain of the guard, wiped his sword, and went his way back to the palace, for the feast was not yet at an end, and he was minded to lose no more of it. At the bidding of big Anna the folk followed him, all save the Egyptians. As they went the women wailed for the death of the Horned One all the way, and when they came into the town they spread abroad the tidings of his death.

When they had gone, forthwith big Anna and the Egyptians stripped the young shepherd, and set about rubbing and kneading his body and his limbs. Four rubbed and kneaded, and when four grew weary other four took their place. So they worked for the space of an hour, but neither did the young shepherd breathe, nor did his heart beat, so that at last they began to say, "We waste our pains; he is surely dead."

But big Anna bade them go on with the work, saying, "If he were dead, then would he be already cold. Moreover, if he die, we shall die also; the Princess hath sworn it."

When they heard this, they said no more that the young shepherd was dead, but strove and strove to awaken him to life.

And in the Eastern sky above the mountains the moon was bright.

For yet another hour they strove; and then one of those who rubbed his body cried out in a joyful voice, "His heart beats." And presently they saw that he breathed.

And they were all of them joyful save the Egyptian; and he said, "I would I knew that he had truly died."

"If he did not die, then is there no death," said big Anna.

The Egyptians rubbed and kneaded the harder; and the heart of the young shepherd beat quicker; and presently he murmured so that they scarcely heard him, "Lo, the shadows in the darkness; why do they run swiftly?"

And big Anna and the Egyptian cried with one voice, "The law is fulfilled."

Then big Anna gave the young shepherd wine, and he choked upon it, for his throat was yet cramped from the rope. But the wine warmed him, and presently he sat up, and gazed at the waters of the lake and shivered, though the night was hot and still.

And the Egyptian put a cloak about him, and big Anna gave him more wine, and asked him how he did; but he said, "Peace, woman."

For a long while he was silent, and they stood about him watching him.

At last he said, "Give me to eat."

And they gave him meat and bread and wine. When he had eaten and drunk, he put on a tunic woven of white wool, which the Egyptians had brought for him; and big Anna combed out his tangled hair, and perfumed it; and it lay smooth on his head. And a young Egyptian gave him a shepherd's pipe, and he put it in his girdle.

Then he rose and said, "Lead me to the Princess, she looks for my coming."

"It is not yet time," said big Anna. "She looks for you at midnight."

The young shepherd sat him down again on the bank, and bidding the others withdraw under the trees, he talked with the Egyptian.

When it was about midnight, big Anna came to him and said that it was now time to go to the palace; and they set out, going slowly, for the young shepherd was bruised.

When they came to the postern in the wall of the gardens of the palace, the young shepherd wrapped his head in the cloak of the Egyptian. And the Egyptian sent his young men to the camp, bidding them make everything ready against their setting out on their journey down the Eastern road, and telling them to take no heed of the soldiers guarding the camp, for he would come presently from the Princess bringing leave to depart.

Then big Anna showed to the soldier who guarded the postern the signet of the Princess, and he let them in. Big Anna would have had the young shepherd and the Egyptian wait on the lawn of the White Image while she went into the palace and got word to the Princess through the brides-woman. But the young shepherd said: "Nay; lead me to her chamber, and I will call to her, for she is awake."

They came, therefor, through the gardens and along the side of the palace till they stood under the chamber of the Princess; and big Anna and the Egyptian stayed among the trees. But the young shepherd came under the casement of the bride-chamber, and called softly to the Princess.

And straightway she came to the casement, and said in a joyful voice: "Is it you, dear love? Is it truly you? I come."

Nor did she speak softly, for she had put the potion which big Anna had sent to her in the wine of the Prince, and he slept soundly.

Then she left her casement, and came quickly and panting down into the garden and ran to the young shepherd, and cried out, "O, the slow hours, and dreadful with fear!"

And the young shepherd put his arms about her and kissed her, and she kissed him many times, and told him how she had feared and trembled.

And the Egyptian called from among the trees that the young shepherd must not tarry, for they must be far down the Eastern road by the break of day.

Then the Princess said, "Whither do you flee, my beloved? When will you come to me again?"

"Farewell, dear love, farewell!"

"I fare forth through the world with the Egyptians," said the young shepherd. "And when I come again I know not; it may not be in a year, nor in twain. But assuredly I will come to you again, for your eyes will draw me to you."

And big Anna and the Egyptian came from among the trees, and big Anna gave to the Princess her signet. The Princess kissed it, and gave it to the young shepherd, saying, "Let it be for a token and a remembrance."

"How should I forget?" said the young shepherd.

Then the Egyptian said, "Come, we must go, and go quickly."

And he and big Anna turned and went through the trees.

Again the young shepherd held the Princess in his arms, and kissed her many times; and she clung to him and wept.

And again, from far away among the trees, the Egyptian called, "Haste, haste."

Then the young shepherd loosed the Princess, and said, "Farewell, dear love, farewell!"

And he went quickly through the trees after big Anna and the Egyptian. Neither did he turn his head, nor look back, fearing lest he should be constrained to return to her.

And the Princess leaned against the wall of the palace and wept bitterly.

But when the young shepherd came into the town, he took the shepherd's pipe from his girdle and began to play the tune of the White Image. And when it rose upon the air, there were cries of affright in houses, and the clatter of barring shutters, and the sound of men and women crying to one another, "Lo, the shepherd! The shepherd who was dead is alive again!"

But the tune was full of moonlight and lazily blinking stars, and warm odours of flowers in the night, and burning lips, and humid eyes ashine, and hushed murmuring voices, and cries of triumph on tall hills. And the shepherd went down the long Eastern road.